D0337205

# IF AT FIRST YOU DO NOT SEE

# For Ken






First published in Great Britain in 1982 by Andersen Press Ltd., 20 Vauxhall Bridge Road, London SW1V 2SA.
This paperback edition first published in 1997 by Andersen Press Ltd.
Published in Australia by Random House Australia Pty., 20 Alfred Street, Milsons Point, Sydney, NSW 2061.  Colour separated in Switzerland by Photolitho AG, Offsetreproduktionen, Gossau, Zürich. Printed and bound in Italy by Grafiche AZ, Verona.

10 9 8 7 6 5 4

British Library Cataloguing in Publication Data available.

ISBN 0 86264 760 6

*This book has been printed on acid-free paper*

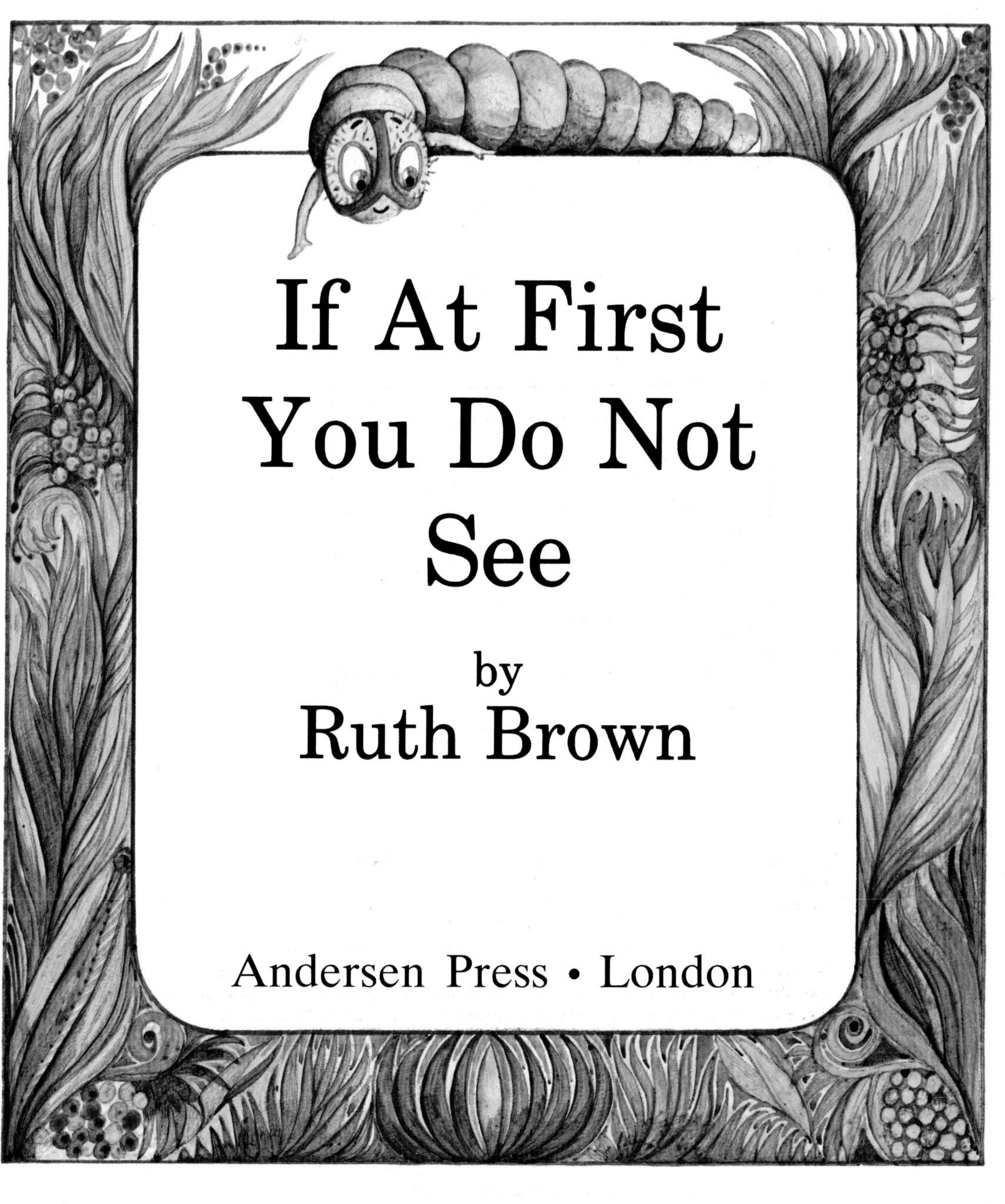

# If At First You Do Not See

by
Ruth Brown

Andersen Press • London

"Now stay here and eat those leaves," said the butterfly to her caterpillars.

"Pooh! How boring," said one caterpillar.
"I want something more exciting. I'm off . . ."

. . . . . And then he saw the strange man.

"Oops! Sorry!" said the caterpillar and crawled away.

"That looks a bit more juicy," said the caterpilla

and started to nibble. . . . . . "Oy! Get off!"

said a voice. "You're eating my hair!" "What?" said the

caterpillar. "Where are you?" . . . . .

"Oooh dear! I'm v-v-very sorry, sir."

And he very quickly climbed off the giant's face.

"Look at that lovely clump of grass . . .

I think I'll taste that," said the caterpillar.

"Get off my nose, you nasty green worm," boomed a voice.

"Wha-a-a-t?" quavered the caterpillar.

saw the two funny men. "But I'm so hungry

– and I can't find anything to eat, anywhere."

"Mmm . . . lovely, cold ice-cream.

I'll have some of that," said the caterpillar.

"Get off! Get off! Go away! Go away!" said two squeaky voices.

"Oh, I am so sorry," said the caterpillar as he

"Oooh, look! A delicious mushroom!

. . . I don't like the look of those two –

I think I'll get away from here . . . quick!"

That definitely looks good enough to eat.

But wait a minute, I'll just have a look to make sure it's safe.

Eeeek! It's a good job I did . . .

"Yum, yum, tasty flowers," said

Touch me and I'll feed you to my pretty bats."

"Aaaaaah!" screamed the caterpillar, and fled.

the caterpillar. "Flowerssss, flowerssss . . ."

hissed a voice. "How dare you mistake me for sissy flowers,

you miserable little grub.

"Oooh! That's more like it – two juicy hamburgers!"

"Pardon me, I'm sure," said the caterpillar.

"You're too ugly to eat anyway," he shouted, as he ran away.

said the caterpillar. "I'm hungry enough to eat both."

"Oy! Clear orf, you 'orrible little creepy-crawly," said a deep voice. "Yeah – clear orf," agreed a second.

"I'm starving, lonely and exhausted," cried the

But by this time . . . . . . . . . . . . .

the poor little caterpillar was fast, fast asleep.

caterpillar. "I'll just have to rest in this straw."

"What are you doing up there?" said a dusty voice.

"Let's have a look at you, little fella."

"You poor little mite," said the scarecrow.